# LITTLE MISS PRINCESS

Roger Hargreaves

Written and illustrated by
**Adam Hargreaves**

EGMONT

Little Miss Princess' father was a King.

And her mother was a Queen.

Which, as I am sure you know, meant that
Little Miss Princess was a Princess.

And because she was a Princess she lived in a castle.

With turrets.

And a moat.

A very big castle.

And because she was a Princess she had lots of people to do everything for her.

People to mow the lawns.

People to cook her breakfast.

She even had people to make her bed.

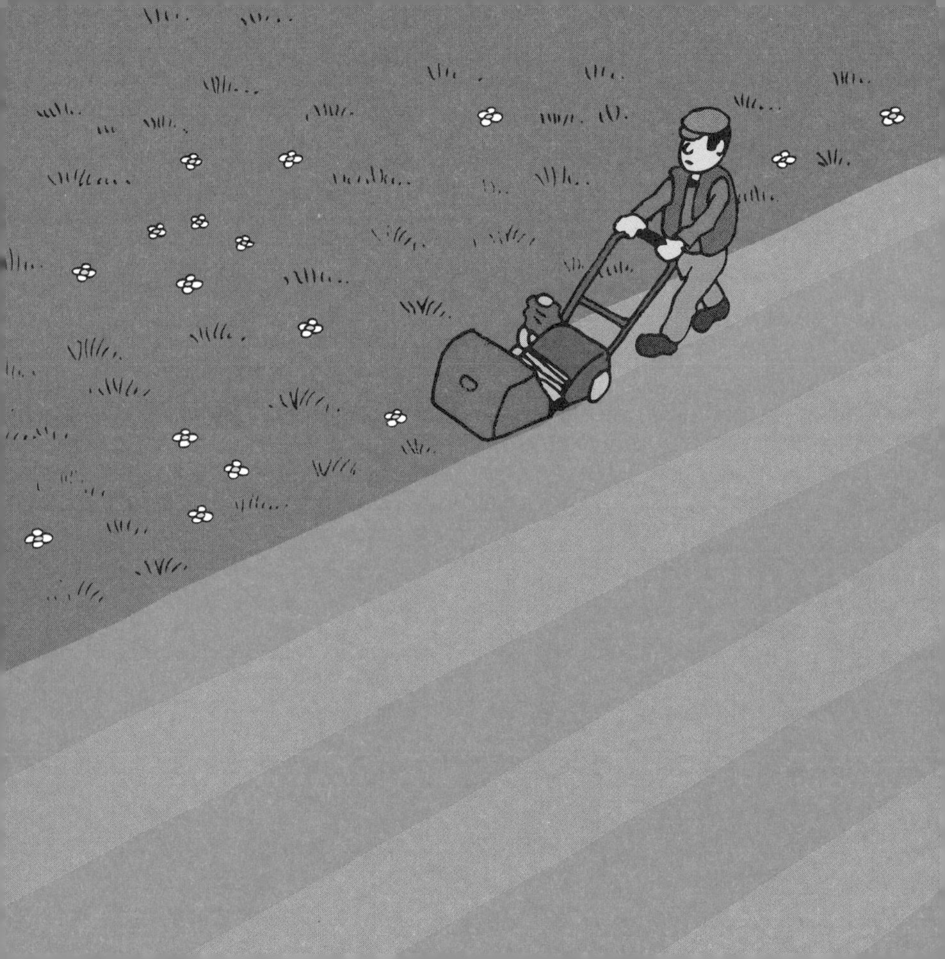

And you would imagine that this would have made her rude and spoilt, but she was a kind and generous and good-hearted Princess.

"I am so lucky to be a Princess, I must spread my luck around," she would say to herself every morning.

And she did this by trying to help people.

She sent a chef to cook meals for Little Miss Sunshine when she heard that Little Miss Sunshine had the flu.

When she overheard Mr Busy complaining how busy he was, she sent a gardener to mow his lawn.

And she sent a maid to Little Miss Neat's house when she heard that Little Miss Neat had worn out her mop.

All of this was very useful and everyone was very grateful, but Little Miss Princess did not feel that she was really doing anything to help.

So when she heard that Mr Bump had broken his leg, she rushed round to his house to see what she could do.

"I haven't got any groceries," said Mr Bump. "You could go to the shops for me."

So Little Miss Princess went to the shops.

But because she was a Princess she had never been shopping.

She went into the bakers.

"Six sausages, please," she said to the baker.

"We don't have any sausages," said the baker.

She went into the butchers and asked for peas.

"We don't have any peas," said the butcher.

And she went into the greengrocers and asked for a loaf of bread.

"We don't have any bread," said the greengrocer.

So she went back to Mr Bump's house with an empty shopping basket.

"The shops have sold out of everything," she explained to Mr Bump.

"Everything?" said a puzzled Mr Bump.

"Yes, the butcher had no peas, the baker had no sausages and the greengrocer said he didn't have any bread."

"Ah," said Mr Bump, realising what had happened. "Why don't you try the supermarket?"

Some time later, Little Miss Princess returned with the shopping. She offered to help put everything away, but because she was a Princess she had never unpacked the shopping.

She put the sausages in the cupboard, the frozen peas in the bread bin, the bread in the drawer and …

… the milk in the oven.

Whoops!

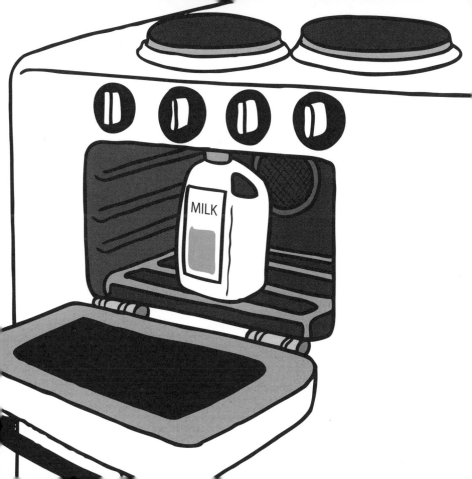

After she had put the shopping away, Little Miss Princess offered to clean Mr Bump's house, but because she was a Princess she had never cleaned anything before.

She dusted the dishes, she polished the sofa and she mopped the carpet.

Oh no!

Little Miss Princess then went upstairs to make Mr Bump's bed, but because she was a Princess she had never made a bed.

Oh dear!

Little Miss Princess then offered to cook supper for Mr Bump, but because she was a Princess she had never cooked a meal before.

For supper they had burnt sausages with burnt potatoes.

She even burnt the peas!

"Oh dear," said Little Miss Princess, throwing the burnt meal away. "I'm just no good at anything."

"Oh, I wouldn't say that," said Mr Bump. "I'm sure you are good at all sorts of things."

"Like what?" sniffed Little Miss Princess.

"I know," said Mr Bump. "Why don't you ring for a pizza?"

"What will that prove?" asked Little Miss Princess.

"Well," said Mr Bump …

" … you are very good at giving orders!"

# Fantastic offers for Little Miss fans!

## Collect all your Mr. Men or Little Miss books in these superb durable collector's cases!

Only £5.99 inc. postage and packaging, these wipe clean, hard wearing cases will give all your Mr. Men and Little Miss books a beautiful new home!

STICK £1 COIN HERE
(For poster only)

## Keep track of your favourite Mr. Men and Little Miss characters with this brilliant collector's poster, now featuring Mr. Nobody!

Collect 6 tokens and we will send you a giant-sized double-sided poster! Simply tape a £1 coin in the space provided and fill out the form overleaf.

**Only need a few Mr. Men or Little Miss to complete your set?** You can order any of the titles on the back of the books from our Mr. Men order line on 0870 787 1724. The majority of orders are delivered in 5 to 7 working days.

---

## TO BE COMPLETED BY AN ADULT

To apply for any of these great offers, ask an adult to complete the details below and send this whole page with the appropriate payment and tokens, to: MR. MEN CLASSIC OFFER PO BOX 715, HORSHAM RH12 5WG

☐ Please send me a giant-sized double-sided collector's poster.

AND ☐ I enclose 6 tokens and have taped a £1 coin to the other side of this page

☐ Please send me ☐ Mr. Men Library case(s) and/or ☐ Little Miss Library case(s) at £5.99 each inc P&P

☐ I enclose a cheque/postal order payable to Egmont UK Limited for £.............................

OR ☐ Please debit my MasterCard / Visa / Maestro / Delta account (delete as appropriate) for £.............................

Card no. ☐☐☐☐ ☐☐☐☐ ☐☐☐☐ ☐☐☐☐ ☐☐☐☐ Security code ☐☐☐

Issue no. (if available) ☐ Start Date ☐☐ / ☐☐ / ☐☐ Expiry Date ☐☐ / ☐☐ / ☐☐

Fan's name:                                                Date of birth:

Address:

                                                           Postcode:

Name of parent / guardian:

Email of parent / guardian:

Signature of parent / guardian

Offer is only available while stocks last. We reserve the right to change the terms of this offer at any time and we offer a 14 day money back guarantee. Please allow up to 28 days for delivery. This does not affect your statutory rights. Offers apply to UK only.
☐ We may occasionally wish to send you information about other Egmont books. If you would rather we didn't please tick this box.